Nuptse & Lhotse
Go to the
West Coast

Jocey Asnong

RMB

Dedicated to
Aven, Hawksley and Delevan:
you make my world fuller than full.
Always explore. Be curious.
And always choose
adventure!

A Sea Full of Stars
Books are never made alone, especially ones starring globe-trotting cats. To my Jamey – thank you for you and all you do to make me laugh, create and dream. To the friends and family I put on hold while I'm in my art cave – thank you for your patience, treats, encouragement, advice and inspiration. An ocean-sized thank you to the team at Rocky Mountain Books, Heritage Group and partners – you have made my wildest dreams come true. And finally, a whale of a hug to everyone who has supported, loved and shared my stories with little curious adventurers over the years. Thank you!

If You Go Down to the Beach Today …
Nuptse and Lhotse's West Coast adventures are completely made up but inspired by two peculiar events. Starfish are disappearing and scientists are trying to find out why. Also, in October 2015, Hurricane Oho, a rare, northeast-tracking super storm pounded the West Coast with waves as high as houses. Perhaps a brave little starfish could have travelled far from home and met two adventurous cats. Anything is possible.

Once upon a time, in a place not very far from here and just down the road from over there, two curious and adventurous cats were starting their day.

THINGS ABOUT NUPTSE
(Nup-see)

- Named after Mount Nuptse, a mountain beside Mount Everest
- A little sister cat
- Loves flowers, jellybeans and making up stories
- A scaredy-cat who is sometimes brave

Nuptse

THINGS ABOUT LHOTSE
(Low-zee)

- Named after Mount Lhotse, a mountain near Mount Everest
- A big brother cat
- Loves climbing, books and solving puzzles
- A courageous cat who is sometimes cautious

Lhotse

FERN

A month and a day after their latest adventure, Nuptse and Lhotse found the most extraordinary thing outside after a storm.

"What can this possibly be?" wondered Lhotse. "Do you think we can eat it?" asked Nuptse. "Oh, no! Please don't eat me! I'm Salish, a purple ochre star."

"A star! Are you from outer space?" asked Nuptse.

"Oh, heavens no. I'm a starfish, from the ocean."

"But how did you get from there to here?" asked Lhotse.

"I was playing hide and seek with my starfish friends when a huge hurricane of wind and waves swept us all up and away. Can you take me back?"

"We sure can!" said Lhotse

"It'll be an adventure!" said Nuptse.

They travelled over mountain passes,

through long tunnels,

over raging rivers,

across farmer's fields, around fruit orchards and arrived at a sparkling city by the sea.

GRANVILLE ISLAND

"I can smell the Pacific Ocean!" said Salish when they arrived at a market near the ocean. "But this isn't my home."

"There must be lots of beaches along this coast. We'll just keep looking," said Lhotse.

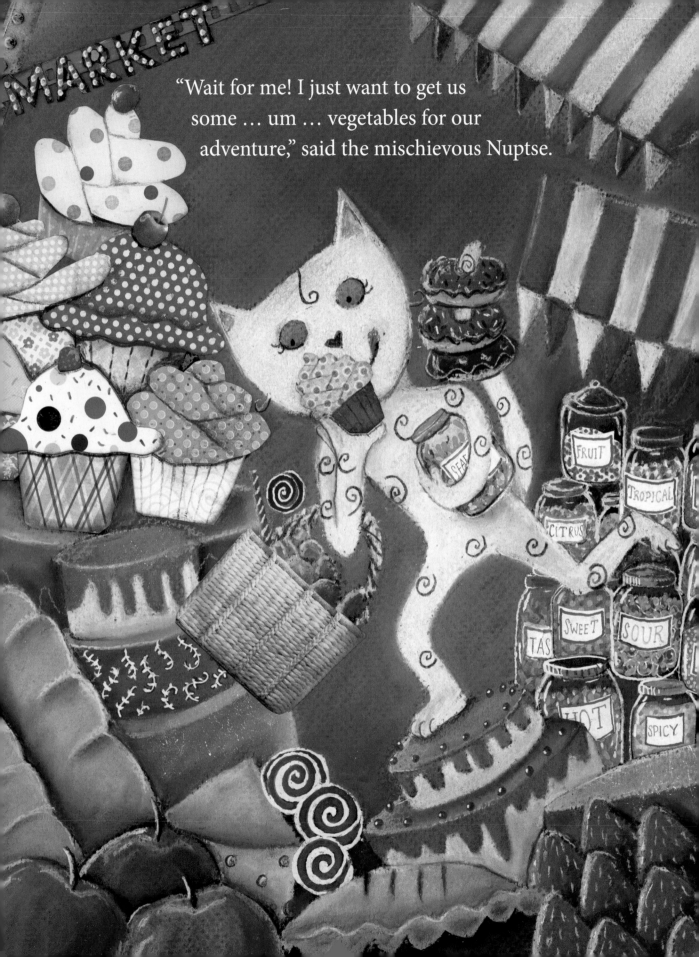

"Wait for me! I just want to get us some … um … vegetables for our adventure," said the mischievous Nuptse.

They ran along the seawall, wandered through Stanley Park, crossed the Capilano River and grinded their way to the summit of Grouse Mountain.

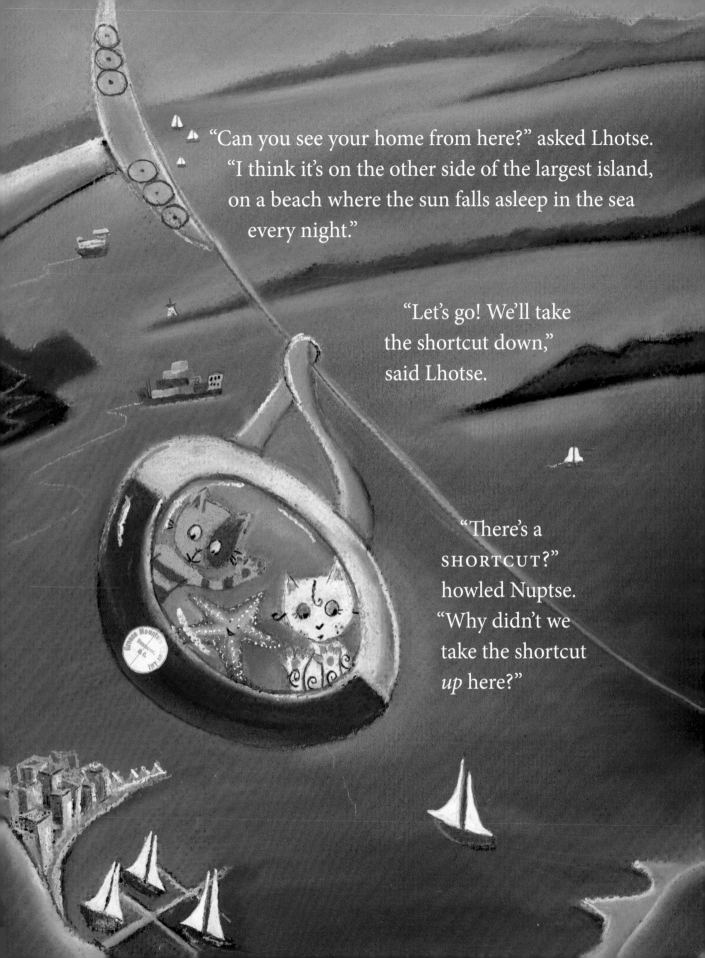

"Can you see your home from here?" asked Lhotse. "I think it's on the other side of the largest island, on a beach where the sun falls asleep in the sea every night."

"Let's go! We'll take the shortcut down," said Lhotse.

"There's a SHORTCUT?" howled Nuptse. "Why didn't we take the shortcut *up* here?"

"Hurry, the ferry is going to leave the harbour soon," said Salish.

"A fairy!" said Nuptse. "What fairytale is she in? I love the one about –"

"Not that kind of fairy!" Salish giggled. "This ferry is a type of boat. We're taking an orca ferry across."

"Isn't an orca a killer whale?" asked Lhotse.

"I'm feeling a little nervous about meeting a whale with that name."

"Orcas are actually members of the dolphin family," replied Salish. "Sometimes they can be quite sneaky, though."

"I've always wanted to swim with dolphins!" said Nuptse.

"I hope you feel the same way about being INSIDE a dolphin!" exclaimed Salish

As they made their way inside, a low booming voice echoed through the orca ferry.

"This is Nanaimo Orca, your resident captain, speaking. Today our cruising depth will be a thousand feet under the sea, and the weather at the bottom is salty

Berths

HUMPBACK

SEI WHALE

FIN WHALE

BELUGA

Whaling Wall

Bridge

Forecastle

Lower Decks

Ballast

with
a chance of jellyfish
blooms and shrimp showers."

"Do you think jellyfish taste like jellybeans?" asked Nuptse.

"I wouldn't try them," Lhotse said, laughing. "They'll sting you!"

"I see a rainbow starfish," said Salish. "Let's get her!"

UNUSUAL THINGS
SOMETIMES FOUND
IN THE OCEAN:

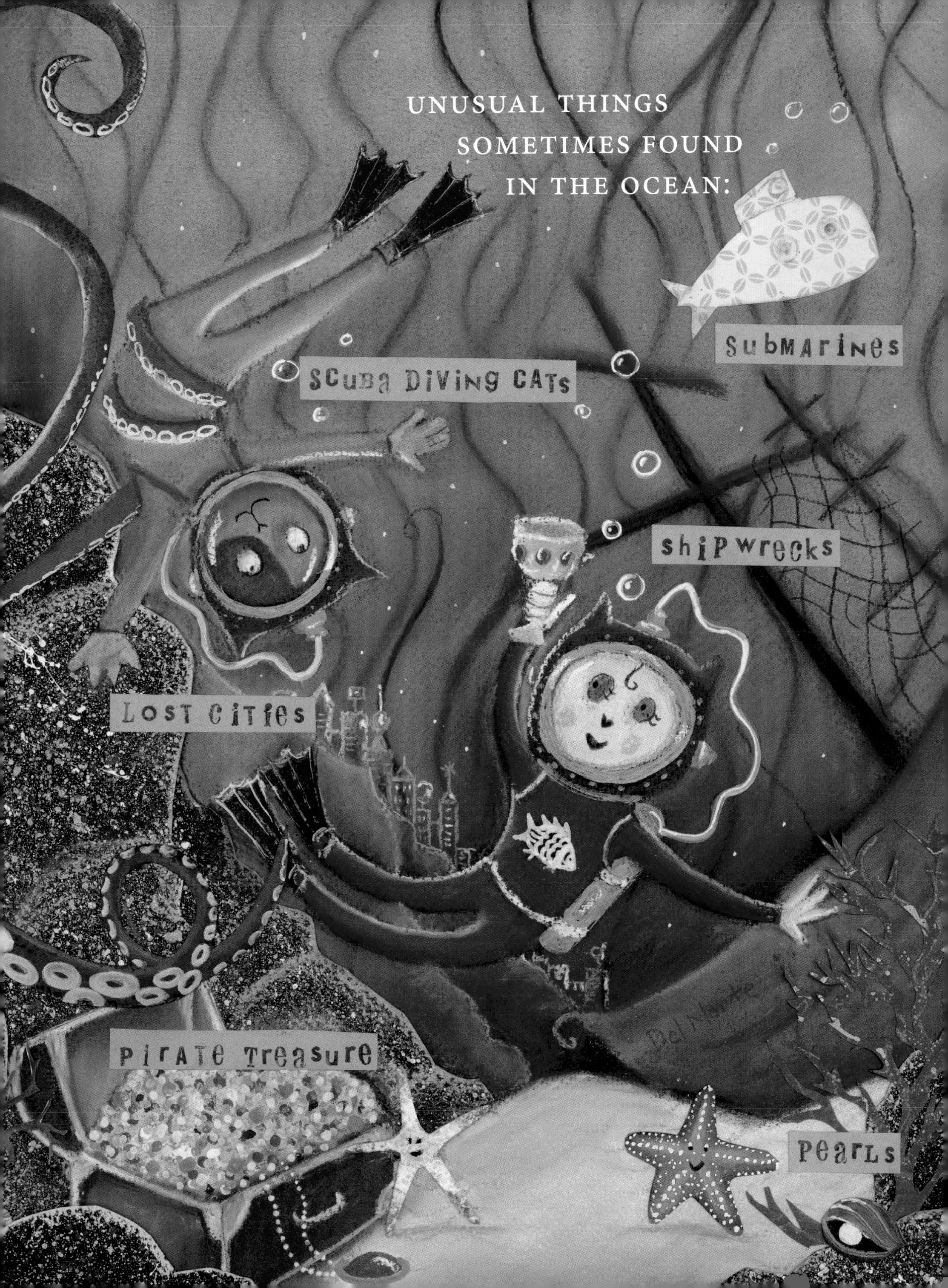

submarines

SCUBA DIVING CATS

shipwrecks

Lost cities

pirate treasure

pearls

"Let's swim to shore and see where we are now," said Lhotse.
    Salish, Rainbow, and the cats flippered, and floated and bobbed up on top.
    "The houses here are swimming!" said Nuptse.
    "They're houseboats," a smiling starfish called. "I'm Cookie,
the starfish. Welcome to Fisherman's Wharf!"

Suddenly, a bucketful of crabs came sprinting sideways down the dock, clicking and clacking their claws and cameras wildly in the air.

"It's a purple ochre starfish!"
"And a rainbow starfish!"
"And a cookie starfish!"
"Get a photo!"
"Get my microscope!"
"Catch them!"
"THEY'RE GETTING AWAY!"

"Follow me into the forest!" said Cookie. "This trail will take us to the beach where Salish comes from."

They galloped from wharf to rainforest, climbing up ladders, sliding down vines, zipping across ravines, balancing along logs, skipping over roots, racing against waves, scrambling up cliffs and jumping over stumps.

"I see an orange sun starfish," exclaimed Salish.

"SUN starfish? Really?" Nuptse snorted. "If I named a starfish I would call it rain starfish or storm starfish or mud starfish or slime starfish … or –"

"But there is a slime starfish!" interrupted Salish. "In fact, there's one, right over there. Come with us, friends, we're going to my home!"

"Oh, no, the tide is too high now, and we can't get across the inlet," said Salish sadly.

"I have an awesome idea!" said Lhotse. He reached inside his backpack.

"You brought our inflatable pool noodles!" Nuptse cheered. "You always bring exactly the right thing for our adventures!"

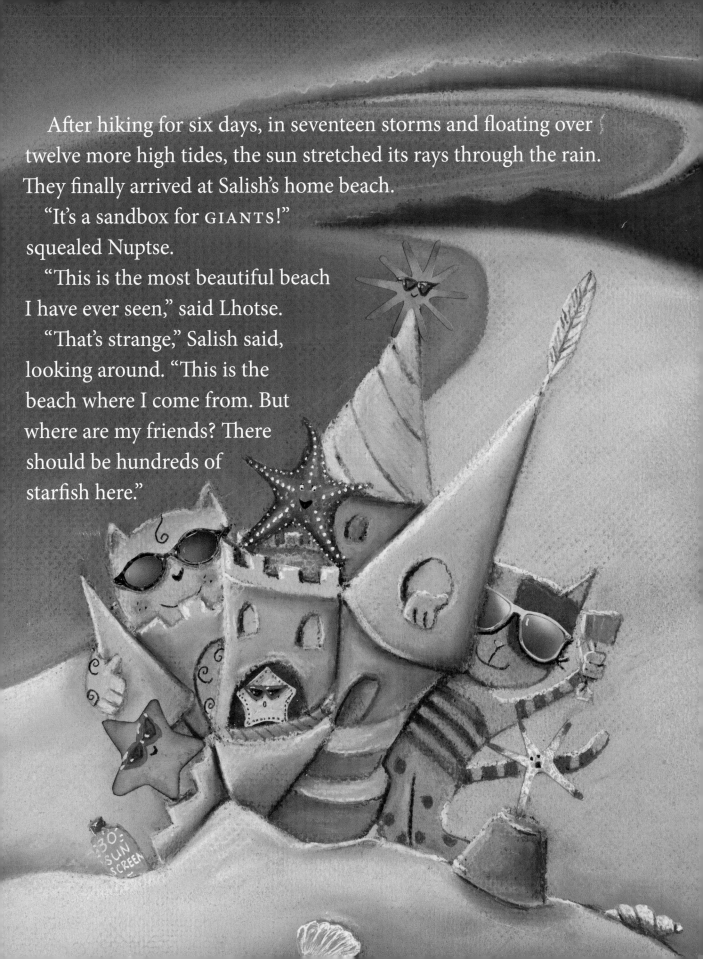

After hiking for six days, in seventeen storms and floating over twelve more high tides, the sun stretched its rays through the rain. They finally arrived at Salish's home beach.

"It's a sandbox for GIANTS!" squealed Nuptse.

"This is the most beautiful beach I have ever seen," said Lhotse.

"That's strange," Salish said, looking around. "This is the beach where I come from. But where are my friends? There should be hundreds of starfish here."

Surf
Slang
Stick: Board
Curls: Big Waves
Sick: Amazing
Backdoor: Entrance
of Wave
Grommet: Beginner
Ankle Busters: small
waves
Hang ten: Surf
with ten toes
Riptide: Dangerous
Side Wave
Ollie: Jump
Shoot: Surf
Gnarly: Difficult

"Hey, grommets, I'm Tofino the surf otter. There might be one spiny red starfish left, shooting gnarly curls by Cat Face Island. Grab a stick and we'll drop in the backdoor once we're past the ankle busters."

"Did he say Cat Face Island?" asked Nuptse.

"Don't ask me, I didn't understand a word he said." Lhotse laughed.

"Check me out," hollered Lhotse. "I'm surfing!"

"Me too!" shouted Nuptse.

"I see a starfish!" said Salish.

"RIDE THE BARREL EVERYONE!" yelled Tofino.

"Here comes a RIPTIDE!"

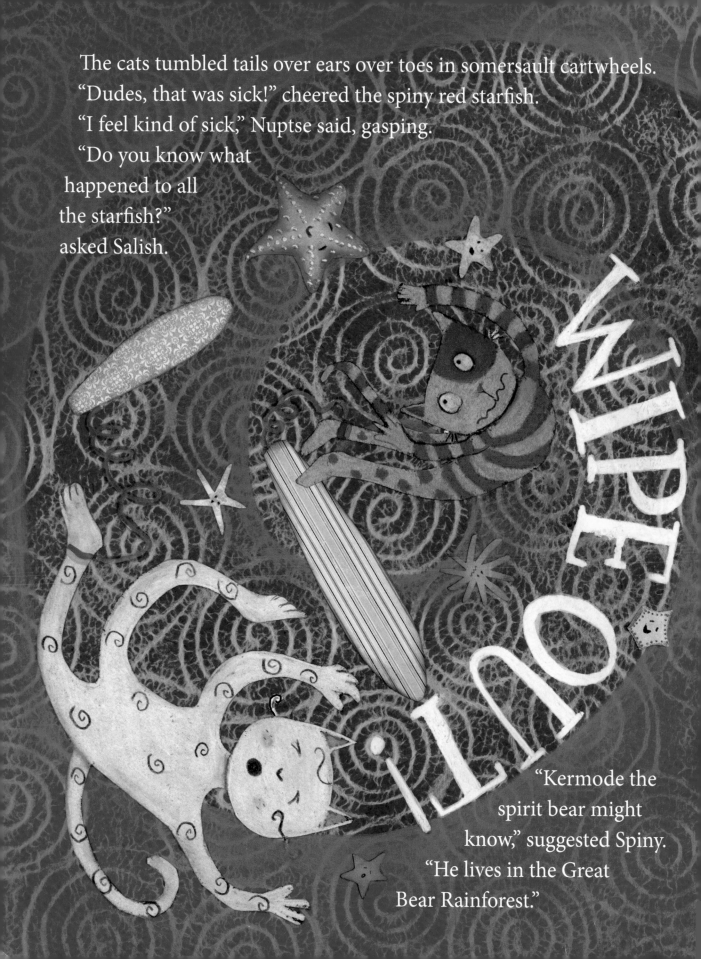

The cats tumbled tails over ears over toes in somersault cartwheels.
"Dudes, that was sick!" cheered the spiny red starfish.
"I feel kind of sick," Nuptse said, gasping.
"Do you know what happened to all the starfish?" asked Salish.

WIPE OUT!

"Kermode the spirit bear might know," suggested Spiny. "He lives in the Great Bear Rainforest."

"How do we get there?" asked Lhotse.

"We'll take the Pineapple Express," said Spiny.

"That sound delicious, is it a fancy drink?" asked Nuptse.

"It's very fancy, for a tropical STORM!" Spiny laughed and then added, "The waves are so big we can ride our boards all the way there!"

"It's so foggy, I can't even see my whisker tips," said Nuptse.

"Can you hear singing?" asked Salish.

"Maybe it's a whale call," suggested Lhotse.

"I think it's a sounding buoy," said Salish. "Those buoys warn sailors that they're near a dangerous shore."

"I'm not a buoy, or a boy,
or even a girl! I'm Bella Coola,
a Sea Wolf MERMAID!"
"We're looking for Kermode,
the spirit bear," said Spiny.
"Go up the river. You'll find him
where the coho salmon fly."

"Did you know that after salmon have spent most of their lives swimming all over the world, they return to the same spot they were born to lay their eggs?" Lhotse asked.

"It's **Dinner Time!!!**" squealed Nuptse.

"DON'T YOU DARE!

I'm Kermode the spirit bear, and that's MINE," roared the biggest, loudest and whitest bear the cats could have ever imagined.

Kermode slurped a salmon like it was a lollipop and then he flipped it, half-finished, into the forest.

"Hey, that's not fair." Nuptse sniffed and said, "You could have shared the rest with us. Trees don't eat salmon, but cats do."

"But these trees do eat salmon! This forest is just as hungry as me, and it takes a lot of fish to keep us both strong. The more I share, the happier the forest is."

cedar THE GREAT LifeGiveR

"Since you seem very smart, do you know where all the starfish have gone?" asked Lhotse.

"Yes! If today is the day before the harvest full moon, we'd better hurry or we'll be late," said Kermode.

"Late for what?" asked Lhotse.

"You'll see!" said Kermode.

121 122 123 124 125 126 127 128 129 130

"This is Haida Gwaii,
the Islands of the People.
The Eagle and Raven
clans have lived here for
thousands of years in
harmony with the land
and ocean," said Kermode.
"We need to find Chief
Raven's longhouse, in the
forest of faces."

SCRATCH

SCRATCH

"I feel like
we are being
watched.
Look! All the
trees have eyes,"
whispered Nuptse.
"Hey! This
pole shows all the
animals we've met on our
adventure. It's telling the
story of everything that has
happened to us," said Lhotse.
He glanced over at Nuptse.
"Um, Nuptse what exactly are
you doing?"
"I'm carving our faces on this
log," said Nuptse. "It's a good
thing I practice so much at home.
I'm like an expert at this!"

"I hear drumming," said Salish.
"What's happening to us?" said Nuptse.
"All of a sudden, I feel very unusual."

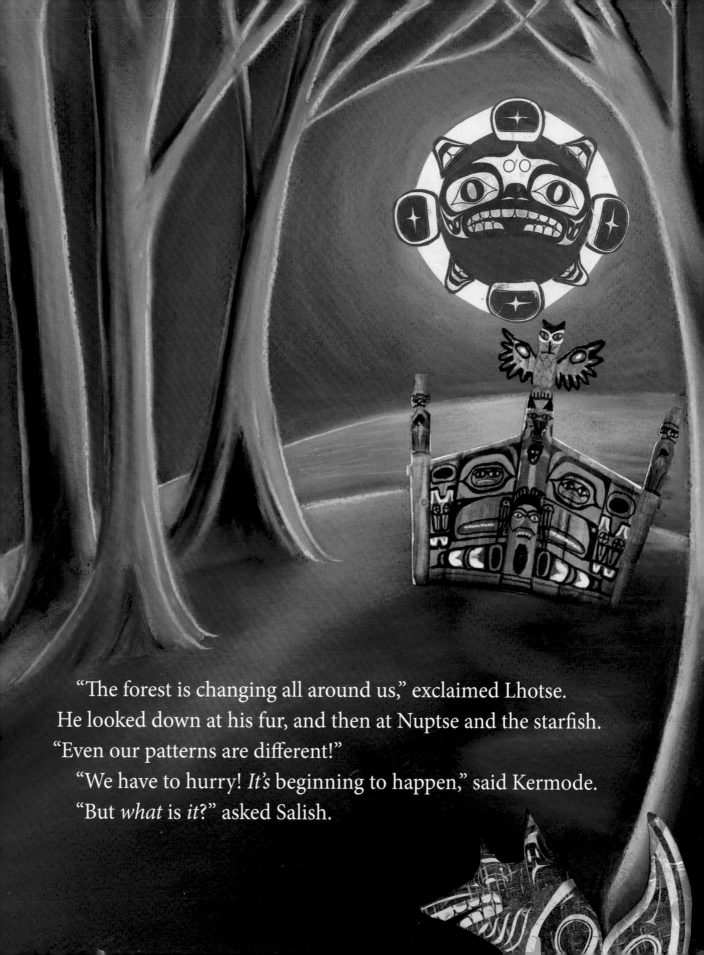

"The forest is changing all around us," exclaimed Lhotse.
He looked down at his fur, and then at Nuptse and the starfish.
"Even our patterns are different!"

"We have to hurry! *It's* beginning to happen," said Kermode.

"But *what* is *it*?" asked Salish.

"Welcome to my FABULOUS FULL MOON POTLATCH PARTY!"

crowed Raven.

"We're going to dance from midnight to morning, and there are presents – *presents* for EVERYONE!

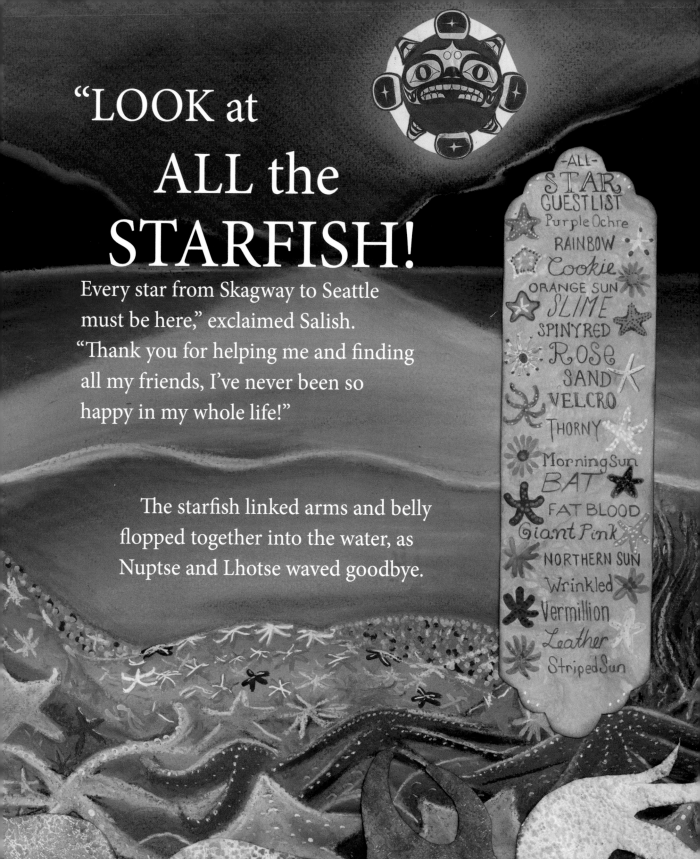

"LOOK at ALL the STARFISH!

Every star from Skagway to Seattle must be here," exclaimed Salish. "Thank you for helping me and finding all my friends, I've never been so happy in my whole life!"

The starfish linked arms and belly flopped together into the water, as Nuptse and Lhotse waved goodbye.

-ALL-
STAR
GUESTLIST
Purple Ochre
RAINBOW
Cookie
ORANGE SUN
SLIME
SPINY RED
ROSE
SAND
VELCRO
THORNY
Morning Sun
BAT
FAT BLOOD
Giant Pink
NORTHERN SUN
Wrinkled
Vermillion
Leather
Striped Sun

"Here are your presents! The Cowichan clan knitted and knotted them just for you so that you will always remember your adventure on the West Coast."

Raven presented the cats with beautiful sweaters.

"Now what did you bring for ME?" he asked, quivering with excitement.

"Thank you. But, well … we're really sorry –"
stuttered Lhotse. "We didn't know –"

"We didn't know which flavour to get you," interrupted
Nuptse as she whipped out a gigantic jar of jellybeans from
her backpack. "But we hope you like these!"

"SEAFOOD JELLYBEANS!"
squawked Raven. "My favourite!
Thank you Nuptse and
Lhotse. This is the best
potlatch ever!"

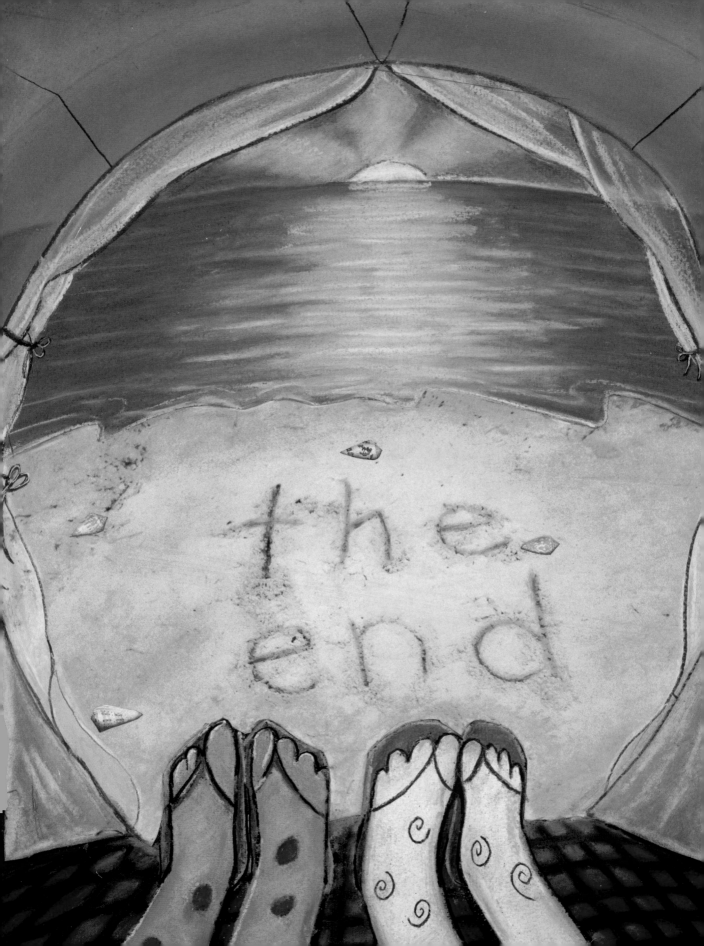